Water Fight!

Michele Martin Bossley

James Lorimer & Company, Publishers
Toronto, 1996

James Lorimer & Company Ltd. acknowledges with thanks the support of the Canada Council and the Ontario Arts Council in the development of writing and publishing in Canada.

Cover illustration: Ian Watts
Models for the cover: Anna Kraulis (left) and Claire McWatt (right)

Canadian Cataloguing in Publication Data

Bossley, Michele Martin
Water fight!

(Sports stories)
ISBN 1-55028-525-4 (bound) ISBN 1-55028-524-6 (pbk.)

I. Title. II. Series: Sports stories (Toronto, Ont.).

PS8553.07394W38 1996 jC813'.54 C96-931314-4
PZ7.B67Wa 1996

James Lorimer & Company Ltd., Publishers
35 Britain Street
Toronto, Ontario
M5A 1R7

Printed and bound in Canada

Contents

For my wonderful twin sons,
Matthew and Jordan,
who entered the world
on June 27, 1996.
God bless you both.

1

Wanted: One New Sister

I glanced quickly up and down the street. No one was in sight. I slowly edged up the front steps of our house and tried the doorknob. It was unlocked. I stifled a groan. That meant my mom was home.

Today was report card day, and I wasn't anxious to face my mother over my marks again. It was like facing off against Wayne Gretzky with a broom handle instead of a hockey stick. There was just no way for me to win.

If I was very, very lucky, I might be able to sneak inside without her hearing me. Then I could quietly bury my report card in the kitchen garbage can. I figured that once it was drowned in mouldy spaghetti sauce, old potato peelings, and other gross leftovers, the chances of my mother wanting to read it were slim.

I said a quick prayer and slowly turned the knob. The door opened with barely a creak. I breathed as softly as I could, slipped off my sneakers, and suddenly came face to face with my mother.

"All right! Hand it over."

"Yikes!" I yelped, my nerves shattered. Mom seemed to have popped out of nowhere. One minute the front hall was empty, the next there she was bellowing in my ear.

"Hand what over?" I said, with a weak attempt at innocence.

Mom crossed her arms over her flannel workshirt. "You know what. The last time report cards were given out, you practically climbed in the basement window to avoid me."

I grimaced and reached into the back pocket of my jeans, where I'd crumpled, scrunched, and wedged my report card into a compact little ball.

"Hey, Mom! Guess what?" Just then my sister Melissa raced through the back door and bounced into the hall. She flashed her own report card and a brilliant, straight-toothed, white smile at my mother.

I sighed. While normally I'd be thankful for the interruption, play-by-play coverage of Melissa's academic greatness didn't strike me as a good idea. For one thing, it would make my report card look even worse; for another, it was really irritating.

"Why, Melissa, this is terrific!" My mother gave Melissa a hug, her face glowing with pride as she reviewed the teachers' comments. "You've brought your science grade up to a ninety-two per cent! You must have worked so hard, honey."

Melissa smiled with false modesty, and I wanted to gag.

Melissa is my older sister, and she's a major pain in the neck. I'm twelve. She's fourteen and absolutely perfect. She's gorgeous without even trying — long, sparkling, pale blond hair; a wide, sparkling smile; big, sparkling grey eyes. It's pretty disgusting. Especially when you compare her to me — dull blond-brown hair, muddy hazel eyes, pasty-pale skin … nothing sparkles about me.

Melissa also gets practically straight A's at school and she's friendly and outgoing in a way that makes everyone pay attention to her, especially my parents. Sometimes I wonder if Melissa and I are really related. Absolutely nothing about me stands out. I'm just a regular kid.

"Josie," Mom interrupted my thoughts. "About that report card of yours…" She held out her hand and steered me toward the kitchen.

Our kitchen, which had pine cabinets and was decorated in cheerful country reds and blues, was usually one of my favourite rooms in the house. But today it felt like a prison. Melissa followed us and leaned her elbows on the slate blue counter top, a self-satisfied smile on her face.

"Would you believe that the computer broke down just as they were about to do the seventh-grade report cards?" I said hopefully, plunking myself down on one of the patchwork-cushioned chairs.

"Nope."

"How about that Jill Lawson accidentally spilled grape juice all over the teacher's desk, and the report cards were on it and all had to be thrown out?"

"Not a chance," my mother said.

"What if I told you the class hamsters got into the report cards and shredded them to make a new nest?"

"Josie!"

"Oh, okay." I sighed and began digging into the pocket of my jeans. I tugged out a fistful of lint and the tightly scrunched wad of paper that was my report card.

Melissa looked at me with distaste. "Gross, Josie!" She wrinkled her nose in disgust. I ignored her and handed the report card to my mother. She unfolded it and began to read.

I waited silently. Mom's lips tightened and creases began creeping up her forehead. That's when I knew I was really in for it. Any time Mom's forehead creased, it was bad news.

She looked up at me, but before she could speak I turned to Melissa, who was still hanging around.

"It's not like you have to listen," I told her.

"I'm not listening," she said innocently. "I'm making myself hot chocolate." She reached into a cupboard, pulled out a tin of cocoa, and pried off the lid with elaborate nonchalance.

"Melissa, go up to your room," Mom said. "You can make hot chocolate in a little while."

"But —" Melissa began to whine but saw the expression on Mom's face and thought the better of it. "Oh, all right," she said, brushing past me impatiently.

When we heard the door to Melissa's room close, Mom finally spoke. "Josie, what's going on? Your grades are even lower than last year."

I stared at my fingernails and shrugged. "I know."

"Your marks in social studies, computers and math aren't great, but a fifty-five per cent in science, and a fifty-two in language arts —" She shook her head. "You're barely passing."

"I know," I whispered.

"What's going on with you, Josie?" Mom asked again. "You're a very bright kid. There's no excuse for these marks." She paused for breath. "Either you're not applying yourself to your studies, or something else is wrong. Is starting junior high too much of a change? Are you having trouble seeing the board? Are you having trouble learning the material? Should Dad and I get you a tutor?"

"No," I said. Oh brother, I thought. Mom's really wound up this time.

"Josie, your whole future depends on your success in school," Mom said. "You have to start thinking about that. How are you going to get into university if you don't …"

I tried to look as though I was listening. It's not that I don't care what my mom thinks, or if she's disappointed in me — actually I care a lot about that — it's just that once she starts lecturing she can go on for hours. The only way to get her to stop is to pretend to be very serious and agree with what she says. If you argue or ask questions, the lecture takes three times as long.

"... from now on you really have to spend more time studying and doing homework. Dad and I will start checking your work every night and helping you if we need to."

I nodded solemnly.

Mom got up and began rummaging around in the pots and pans. "You'd better go start whatever homework you have for tonight," she said above the clatter. "I want to see what you can get done before supper."

I breathed a quiet sigh of relief and escaped to my room. Instead of opening my textbooks, I flopped down on the bed, rolled on my back, and looked up at my favourite poster, which I had tacked on the ceiling.

It was a wash of different blues painted to look like water splashing, and right in the middle a girl in a red bathing suit was swimming. The artist had captured her straining to win — her face had a powerful, determined look. Down at the bottom a drawing of a gold medal strung on a red-and-white ribbon was under the words, "Reach for your dreams."

That was my dream. The gold medal. Someday the name Josie Waterson would be written up as the fastest swimmer ever to race in the Olympics. And Worlds. And Nationals.

I love swimming. I always have. Somehow I just feel free in the water, like there's nothing I can't do.

Of course, that's not always true. Sometimes, no matter how hard I try, I don't compete at my best. But my coach says that hard work and determination often outweigh talent, and I can work harder in the pool than anybody.

I rolled off the bed with a thump. My homework lay on the floor, scattered and disorganized where it had fallen out of my knapsack. I wished I could just ignore it, but I knew Mom would really have a fit if I didn't at least do something.

The weird thing is, I don't mind school that much. It just seems like no matter what I do, Melissa does it better. If I get a B on a test, Melissa gets an A. That's the way it's always been. I used to try really hard to get better grades than Melissa, but it always seemed like she was the best. And even if I did get an A, my parents just took it for granted, like somehow Melissa's genius genes had naturally been passed down to me, and it wasn't worth making a fuss over. Either that, or Melissa would show up with some soccer trophy or blab about her next ballet recital or something, and she would get all the attention anyway.

Sitting on the floor, I flipped open my math textbook and began writing down the problems. I'd finished three when Melissa stuck her head in the door.

"Get in trouble?" she asked.

"Nope," I lied. I scribbled down problem four and didn't glance up. Nosy, I thought. It was none of her business if I got in trouble.

Melissa paused. "Well, anyway, it's your turn to set the table, and Mom says supper's ready."

"I'll be down in a minute."

"Mom said now."

"I said, in a minute." I looked up, irritated.

"You don't need to yell," Melissa said. "I'm only doing what Mom asked me to."

"Yeah, like always."

"What's that supposed to mean?" Melissa demanded.

"Nothing."

"What did you mean?" she insisted.

I threw down my pencil and stood up. "Okay, if you really want to know," I said. "Nobody else gets any attention around here, because you, Little Miss Terrific, always have to outdo everybody. I'm so sick of hearing about how great you are!" I screwed my face up into a grimace and mimicked, "Melissa, Melissa, Melissa. Oh, how wonderful you are."

Surprise and hurt flashed across Melissa's face. Then anger replaced them. "I can't help it if my marks are better than yours," she said with an irritating smirk.

"You are such a jerk sometimes!"

"And you're such a brat. Why don't you grow up for a change?"

"Why don't you shut up for a change?" I yelled.

"Fine!"

"Good!" I kicked the door shut as Melissa flounced out.

"Ow!" Melissa's shriek echoed in the hallway.

I yanked the door open and watched as Melissa put on an act that would have won her an Academy Award. She howled and held the back of her heel, limping and groaning as my mother barrelled up the stairs.

"What happened now?" she asked.

"She," said Melissa, pointing at me with a dramatic gesture, "deliberately picked a fight just because she's in a bad mood about her stupid report card and then slammed the door shut on me. Look at this!" Melissa sniffled. Her sock had a tiny stain of blood near the heel, and when she peeled the sock back a scrape the size of a pea was revealed. "The bottom edge of the door practically ripped my foot right off."

My mother really lost her temper. "Josie!" she yelled. "How many times do I have to tell you not to slam doors! Especially when someone's standing in them!"

"Yeah!" Melissa added.

I was beginning to feel like an absolute slug, even though I knew Melissa was faking most of the pain. "I —"

"There's no reason for you to take your anger out on your sister," Mom said, gritting her teeth.

"But — !"

"Not another word out of you. You can stay up here and come down for your own dinner later. I need some time to cool off, and so do you." Mom swivelled around, nudged Melissa ahead of her and marched downstairs.

I leaned against the doorway and sulked. Everything was so unfair. I hadn't meant to hurt Melissa, but it was so easy to get ticked off when she acted like such a jerk. And on top of it, my mother didn't even care about my side of the story.

But then, I'm beginning to feel like that's normal. It seems like Melissa is the big star in our family, while I'm stuck somewhere backstage.

2

Plunging In

My alarm clock buzzed at 5:15 the next morning, but I was already awake. Sometimes it was hard to leave my warm, cozy bed for the prospect of jumping into a freezing cold pool, but not this morning. This morning I couldn't wait to get there.

After last night, I was looking forward to the workout. I still felt mad about my fight with Melissa, and angry that no one would listen to me. I knew from experience that swimming off some of the frustration would make me feel better.

I yanked on a pair of old sweatpants and a ratty T-shirt, grabbed my swim bag, and tiptoed softly down the hall.

"Dad?" I tapped softly on my parents' bedroom door. "You up?"

A hollow groan answered me. After a few snuffling and shuffling sounds, my father appeared at the door.

"Yeah, I'm up," he yawned. "Let's go."

I grabbed a banana from the fruit bowl on the kitchen counter and a granola bar. I can never make it through a morning practice without at least something in my stomach, and there's never time for a full breakfast. I'd have that later, when I came home to change before school.

"So, I hear there were a few fireworks last night," Dad said casually as he backed the car out of the driveway. He flicked the windshield wipers on against the sleet-filled November snow. I glanced out the window at the soggy white lawns, and the dripping trees, black in the early morning darkness.

"Yeah, a few," I answered finally. My dad tends to lecture me less than my mom, but demands more results. He works for an advertising agency, and performing under tight deadlines and producing results are his specialty.

"Everything under control?" he asked as we approached the community centre. "Did you talk it out?"

"I guess so," I said.

Dad nodded and pulled up in front of the swimming pool. "Good. Have fun at practice."

"Okay." I climbed out of the car and hurried into the warmth of the building. It doesn't matter what season it is in Calgary, five-thirty A.M. feels cold and shivery year-round, and the icy snowfall made it worse.

I took a deep breath, automatically relaxing as the sharp smell of chlorine hit my nose. I'm so used to everything about the pool — the wet tiled floor, the lukewarm showers, the rows of yellow lockers — it seems more like home than my own bedroom.

I changed quickly, yanking on an old faded blue swimsuit, then a red chlorine-eaten suit over top. This might seem strange, but for swimmers it's totally ordinary. You wreck so many suits when you swim every day, one way to make them last longer is to double up with a couple old ones that would be too see-through to wear on their own. I grabbed my swim bag, shoved my clothes into my locker, and hurried out on deck. It was almost time to get into the pool, and I still had to stretch and run through my sets of sit-ups and push-ups.

"Morning, Josie." My coach Dale waved from the big wipeable board where he was writing the workout sets for everyone in erasable black felt pen.

"Hi, Dale," I called. I took a vinyl mat from the hooks on the wall, sat down to stretch my shoulders and legs, and watched Dale write the rest of the workout. His carrot red hair sat in stubborn waves, except where it was too short to be anything but bristles, and his freckles showed against his skin like brown paint spatters. I liked the way he looked — athletic and no-fuss.

"So, how's it going this morning?" Dale capped his pen and walked over to me.

"Good," I said. It was sort of a lie, but not totally. As far as swimming went, I felt fine.

"We're going to work on stroke improvement this morning. We have that invitational meet next month, and I think you could do really well. I want you to concentrate on fly, especially. That could be your best stroke if you work at it, Josie, and not many people can race fly well."

I groaned. "I know. That's because it's so hard!"

Dale just grinned. Butterfly stroke, or fly as everyone calls it, is the toughest stroke to learn. It takes a long time to get it just right, so you don't waste a lot of energy flopping and flailing around like a fish with heartburn.

"Hop in the water when you're finished your push-ups, and I'll work with you after the warm-up."

"I've already done the push-ups," I said, an innocent smile on my face.

Dale wagged a finger at me. "No, you haven't. I've been watching."

I laughed and began the first set. I would never skip push-ups before practice because I know how important they are for building strength, but I love to tease Dale and see if he can catch me trying to fool him. He always does.

Some of the kids don't like Dale because he's a very firm coach. He doesn't let us goof off during practice, unless it's a special occasion, and he takes swimming as a sport very seriously. When somebody does waste time at practice, he yells a lot, and once he sent a swimmer home for being a jerk. But Dale and I get along fine because he knows how important swimming is to me, and I know he wants to make me the best swimmer I can possibly be.

"Come on, Josie, get in!" Dale gestured toward the pool.

I whipped off the last set of push-ups, tucked my hair under my cap, and dove in. Ross, my best friend in the swim club, was already in the pool, and he splashed playfully at me.

"About time you got here," he said, shaking water from his stiff brush cut. Ross never bothers to wear a swim cap, so he always looks like he has a head full of bristles. I call it his chlorine haircut.

"I'll still do more laps than you, even if I am late," I retorted, adjusting my goggles.

"Hah. In your dreams."

"Ross! Get going!" Dale bellowed from the edge. "Four times 400 IM kick."

Ross grumbled under his breath as he reached for a flutter board. I dove under the water and began the warm-up, which was a typical one — 400 metres freestyle (that's sixteen lengths), then four times 200 metres IM stroke. That means the first 200 metres (eight lengths) are butterfly, then the next 200 are backstroke, the next are breast stroke, and the last are freestyle. That's a total of forty-eight lengths, just for the warm-up.

I like to shock people by telling them how many lengths of the pool I swim at practice. Their eyes bug out, and they say things like, "Wow, that's incredible" or "How do you do that?" It makes me feel kind of important. But the truth is, you get used to swimming that much, and it doesn't seem like such a big deal. When we have heavy training, a few months before the competitions begin, we sometimes swim around

300 lengths for a two-and-a-half-hour afternoon practice. That's 7.5 kilometres.

But for morning practices, it's never as hard. We only have an hour and a half, so Dale usually has us do a good warm-up, then work on drills to strengthen our muscles or increase speed, or else concentrate on stroke improvement. In spite of what people might think, there's a precise technique to each stroke, and learning it takes a lot of practice. When people act amazed at how far I swim, they don't realize that it isn't as hard for me because I'm learning how to swim each stroke very fast without wasting a lot of energy.

I reached for the starting block as I came up to the edge on the last 200 and pulled myself part way out of the water.

"Good work, Josie," Dale commented as he walked past. "You're really getting up some speed today."

"Thanks," I puffed. I wiped the steam from my goggles and lifted them back so they rested on my forehead. I felt a tug on my ankle and looked back.

"Hey, lazy!" Ross teased. "I'm almost finished the 400 kicks. Caught up, yet?"

"Like you're really done," I said scornfully. Ross is the worst kicker — he gets all his speed from his thick-set upper body. "You're probably on, oh, the second length."

"Nope, the third," Ross grinned. Then, avoiding Dale's reproving stare, he turned and pushed off, deliberately splashing me with his flutter kick.

I smiled and sank back into the water, feeling its coolness against my hot face. When I came up, Dale was standing over me.

"Josie, I want you to skip the 400 kicks and come over to the far lane so we can work on fly. The rest of the team is doing drills, so I have a little bit of time just for you."

I smiled. Dale had a way of making me feel special. He actually treated all the swimmers like that, but it felt good to be appreciated. At least there was someone who believed I could really accomplish things.

"Okay," Dale knelt at the edge when I had swum over. "Try and focus on the rhythm of the stroke. Pay attention to the downward stroke on the kick. That's where you get the most power."

I nodded and began to swim a length. I could see Dale walking beside me on deck, studying every move I made. I tried extra hard to do everything right, but he still had more corrections for me.

"Better, Josie, but that kick could still have more strength. Try to think of flicking your feet at the end. Also, stretch your arms a little more before they enter the water. You'll get more speed with a longer extension."

"Okay," I said, concentrating, and began to swim another length.

By the time practice was over, I was exhausted. Dale had only spent about fifteen minutes correcting me, just until the rest of the team was finished the kicking drills, but then everyone worked on stroke improvement together. I kept remembering Dale's corrections as I swam length after length of fly.

My arms felt loose and wobbly as I hauled myself out of the pool. My legs were limp and tingly. But I smiled as I walked into the locker room. I had never felt so good.

3

A Scientific Suggestion

"Hey, Josie," my best friend Delaney Peters poked me in the back. She sat right behind me in science class. "You look totally wiped out. What's the matter?"

I yawned. "Tough practice this morning, that's all."

Delaney's brown eyes looked sympathetic and she nodded, making her black ponytail bounce. She understood about swimming. She should. I tell her every single detail about practices and competitions all the time.

"All right, everyone. Settle down, please." Our science teacher, Mr. P., motioned for silence. Mr. P.'s real name is Mr. Panagopoulos, but he asked us on the first day of school just to call him Mr. P. He's funny. He said we'd waste too much class time if everybody tried to pronounce his name every time he asked a question.

"Today we're going to talk about plant and animal cells, and how they're different," Mr. P. said.

I stifled a groan. I hadn't finished my homework, even after my mother's huge lecture the day before. I was just too tired, and knowing I had to get up early, well, it was easy to skip reading my science chapter. I had finished the worksheets, though.

Mr. P. glanced around the room. "Josie, can you tell us something about plant cells?"

Just my luck. "Uh ... well," I stalled, thinking frantically. "they're ... um ... kind of green."

Mr. P. shot me a disappointed look. "Not always, Josie. But sometimes, yes, they're green. Can anyone else add to that?"

The discussion went on without me. Mr. P. didn't call on me again. It was obvious I hadn't finished all the work, so I wasn't surprised when he stopped by my desk while everyone was writing down lab instructions and discreetly asked to see me at the end of class.

Just before the bell rang, Mr. P. stood up at the front of the room.

"Okay, everyone. Before it's time to go, I want to let you know about the school science fair. It's coming up next month, and I'd like to encourage all of you to enter. Everyone who does will get extra credit toward their science grade, which some of you could definitely use." Mr. P. grinned at us, but I lowered my eyes. I knew I was one of the people he was talking about. "Winners in each grade will be chosen, and they get to go on to compete at the city's annual science fair, which is a lot of fun. So please think about entering."

The bell blasted through the halls. Students hurried to grab their books and get their full five minutes of freedom before the next class. That's one nice thing about junior high, you get to see your friends in the hall every forty minutes. But there's no recess. That's kind of a drag.

"Don't wait," I said to Delaney, who was standing behind me. "Mr. P. wants to talk to me, and you'll be late."

Delaney nodded knowingly. "Good luck."

"Thanks." I gathered up my science homework and my courage and approached Mr. P.'s desk.

He was writing something in a notebook and didn't look up. I cleared my throat.

He tore the sheet of paper out of the notebook, folded it, and handed it to me. "Here Josie, I want you to give this to your mom or dad, have them sign it, and bring it back."

"What is it?" I asked nervously.

He smiled. "Nothing to get you in trouble. It's just my recommendation that you join the science fair this year. You really need the extra credit to boost your grades, Josie."

I swallowed. "I know."

"Josie …" Mr. P. hesitated. "Is something wrong? Is there anything bothering you?"

I felt startled. "No … not really, I guess."

"Well, if you should ever want to talk about anything, science or otherwise, I'm here, okay? Or there's Ms. Valdez in the Guidance Department, if you'd rather."

"No, I'm okay," I said, bewildered.

"I know." Mr. P. smiled. "It's just that I know you're a very intelligent girl. I can tell. And when an intelligent girl like you isn't doing well in my class, there's usually a reason. I'm just saying that if that reason is anything else besides simply not doing your homework …"

I blushed.

"… then I'm here to help. Okay?"

"Okay," I said.

"Good. Now get your parents to sign the note, and please think about the science fair. It'll be fun."

"Okay," I repeated. I knew Delaney wanted to join the science fair — she'd been bugging me about it already. I had never wanted to enter before, but Mr. P. made it sound pretty good, until his next words threw a chill over everything.

"I had your sister Melissa for science when she was in seventh grade," Mr. P. said. "She had a terrific entry that year." He winked at me. "That's how I can tell that you're such a smart kid. I figure it must run in the family."

I nodded stiffly. My throat seemed suddenly tight.

"All right, Josie, you'd better get going to your next class, or you'll be late. See you tomorrow."

"Thanks, Mr. P.," I said dully. My sneakers felt heavy as I walked out the door and started down the hall. I didn't care if I was late.

Why did everyone think that I should be just like Melissa? Even at school, everyone compared me to her. I suddenly felt so angry that I crumpled Mr. P.'s note in my palm. For a minute, when Mr. P. talked about the science fair so enthusiastically, I thought I might want to enter. But not now. Not if everyone was going to look at my project and wonder how the brilliant and beautiful Melissa Waterson could end up with such a dorky, stupid little sister.

4

Me and My Big Mouth

"Hi, Soggy," Melissa greeted me as I entered the kitchen.

"Hi." I shrugged off my jacket, threw down my swim bag and collapsed into a kitchen chair. "Is there any dinner left? I'm starving."

"Yeah, help yourself." Melissa gestured toward the stove.

Oh joy, I thought, peering into the pots. I get to load up on steamed spinach and Brussels sprouts, both of which I hated. There was one pork chop left and a tiny spoonful of mashed potatoes.

"Why didn't anyone save me some potatoes?" I asked in annoyance.

"Hey, first come, first served," Melissa said. She didn't bother to look up from her homework.

She doesn't care, I thought. She had a nice, filling meal, while I was slaving away in the pool. She was probably the one who hogged all the potatoes, too. Melissa loved mashed potatoes.

"Thanks a lot, Pig," I said.

Melissa looked up, an irritated expression on her face. "Hey, can I help it if you miss dinner all the time because of your stupid swim practice?"

"Yeah, well, you'll wish you weren't so selfish when your butt starts to balloon from eating too much."

Melissa just smiled in an annoying way. "That doesn't seem to be a problem." She extended her shapely legs from under the table and admired them.

I made a barfing noise. "Pardon me if I don't join the Melissa-Is-So-Wonderful Admiration Society. I happen to know what you're really like."

"Then you should be a charter member." Melissa went back to her books.

I simmered as I choked down mouthfuls of spinach. I know it's good for you, but I hate that slimy feeling of it squishing around in my mouth. I finally resorted to swallowing it whole.

"Would you mind not eating like a starving rhinoceros? Some of us are trying to concentrate."

"Some of you should go somewhere else, then," I retorted.

Melissa muttered as she packed up her stuff. "Just because you never do any homework ..."

I glared at her. "I do homework."

"Yeah? When?" Melissa challenged. "The last day of school?"

"No, all the time." But that was a lie, and Melissa knew it.

"Hah," she said.

"I do!" I protested.

"That's why you're practically flunking science, right?"

That comment stung. "It just so happens, Ms. Big Shot, that I'm in the science fair this year," I blurted. "I have a terrific idea for a project, and I'm going to win. So there!"

Melissa stared at me. Then she grinned. "I'll believe it when I see it," she said.

"You'll see it," I insisted. "And it'll be better than your dumb idea, whatever it is."

Melissa didn't bother to reply. She just walked out of the kitchen.

I groaned inwardly. Me and my big mouth. Why had I said such a stupid thing? Now I was roped into entering the science fair whether I wanted to or not. I fished into my pocket for the crumpled note that Mr. P. had sent home with me and stared at it gloomily. There wasn't any need for a creative disposal idea now. I might as well get Mom to sign it.

I choked down a soggy Brussels sprout and grimaced. I was about to give up on dinner and reach for some ice cream, when there was a knock on the back door. My friend Delaney stuck her head in. "Anybody home?"

"Hi, Dee," I said, rinsing my plate. "Come on in."

"I called, but I got your Mom on call-waiting on the phone. She said to just come over."

"That's good, because I have something to tell you."

Delaney stared at me curiously. "What?"

"Well," I took a deep breath. "We're joining the science fair."

"Really?" Delaney squealed, grabbing my shoulder. "That's terrific! But since when?" She released me. "I thought you didn't want to."

"I didn't. But now I have to." I explained the whole story.

"Josie, you doorknob," Delaney said. "How come you told Melissa you'd beat her? She's won first place for her grade almost every year since kindergarten."

I set my lips stubbornly. "I'm just as smart as she is, and I'm going to prove it."

"But you don't need to prove it. Everyone already knows you're smart."

"No, they don't. My mom and dad think I'm an idiot, compared to her. They never notice anything I do. It's always 'Melissa this' and 'Melissa that' around here."

Delaney sighed. "Josie, there are some totally fantastic things about you that you never even notice because you're so busy being jealous of Melissa."

"I'm not jealous."

"Okay. But listen. You're a great swimmer. You're one of the fastest swimmers in your age group, and I've never known anyone with that kind of dedication before. You're going to make it to the Olympics someday, Josie. I just know it. You're going to win that meet next month, for sure. And you have a great sense of humour. Since when have you ever heard Melissa make a joke that cracks up the whole class? You do that all the time, even when you don't mean to." Delaney paused for breath.

I shrugged. "I guess so."

"And you're nice to everyone. Everyone knows Melissa, but she can be kind of snobby sometimes, you know."

"Yeah, I know," I said. I was surprised that I felt a twinge of protectiveness toward Melissa. It was okay for me to talk about Melissa's rotten personality, but for some reason I didn't like it when anyone else did. I changed the subject.

"Dee, thanks, but you still don't understand. It's my parents who really need to wake up. Except for yelling at me, I don't think they even notice that they have a second daughter." I gave her a wry smile.

Delaney was silent.

"So that's why I want to have a great science entry. I want to beat Melissa, just to shut her up, but if we win, my parents will have to notice me. Okay?"

She nodded. "Okay."

"So let's get started. We need a totally top-secret, terrific idea. One that will blow everyone else's project away," I said.

"All right!" Delaney slapped me a high-five and we grinned at each other.

5

Disasters with Laundry

Darn it, Melissa!" I muttered as I tugged at my swimsuit. The two of us are supposed to do the family's laundry as part of our Things-to-Do-Around-the-House-to-Get-Your-Allowance List. Melissa never forgets to do it, but she also never remembers how to wash my swimsuits, even though I've told her a million times. I've even asked her to just leave them out and I'll wash them myself, but she won't, and then she wrecks them. Sometimes I think she does it on purpose.

She was responsible for one of my most embarrassing moments ever. Have you ever tried bleaching lycra? Don't. It says not to right on the label, but once Melissa did it anyway. I wore the suit and it practically fell apart on me as soon as I got in the pool.

"Arrgghh!" I looked at myself in the locker-room mirror. Melissa had really outdone herself this time. She usually can't shrink my lycra suits, but today I was wearing my "paper" suit. Paper suits aren't really made of paper; they're a thin, not-very-stretchy suit that feels crumply when you touch it. We wear them for competitions only, and they're very tight. The idea behind this kind of suit is that it glues itself to your body, cutting down any water resistance when you race.

The problem is, they're unbelievably tight to begin with, and now, thanks to Melissa's brilliant washing techniques, mine was about four sizes too small.

I sighed. Dale had asked us to wear our paper suits today because we were going to practise relays in a mock competition. The invitational meet was now only two weeks away, and he wanted to record our best possible times and compare them to the last meet, to see if we were improving.

I surveyed myself in the mirror. The suit squeezed around me like the skin on a sausage, but it was the only one I had, so it would have to do. I picked up my swim bag and hurried out on deck.

Dale was handing out stapled stacks of photocopies. I took one and edged into the back of the group.

"Okay, everyone. These are your information sheets about this year's club fees and fund-raisers. Be sure to give them to your parents, please. It's very important that we get organized early this year because costs have gone up." Dale stacked the leftover sheets on his clipboard and surveyed the group. "All right. Jump in and do a quick 400 freestyle to warm up. We're going to conduct this as much like a competition as possible, so please stretch out your shoulders and legs before racing and give it your best shot. Teams are as follows ..."

He began reading off the boys relay teams, so I glanced over the information sheet. I was surprised to discover that my club fees had more than doubled since last year. It was partly due to the fact that I was training a lot more, and of course that was more expensive, but pool bookings, competition fees and transportation, and required items like competition swimsuits and caps (I would need a new swimsuit for sure!) had all gone up in price.

Dad is going to have a fit, I thought as I tucked the papers into my swim bag. *He's always complaining about how much things cost — this would probably send him through the roof.*

"Josie," Dale said, "you're leading off the 4 by 100-metre freestyle relay. Your team is yourself, Beth, Lisa, and Joanne.

We'll be doing some individual events after, including 200 fly for you, okay?"

"Sure," I said.

"All right, then warm up and stretch out. We'll start in about ten minutes." Dale walked away and began setting up the flag banners that stretch across each end of the pool for backstrokers so they know when they're nearing the edge.

Jeepers, my suit was tight! I tugged at it surreptitiously and pulled on my swim cap. I adjusted my goggles and dove into the pool.

The water engulfed me in a cold rush. *Brrrrr!* I began to swim as fast as I could to get warm. My swimsuit was irritating. It kept creeping up my behind as I swam, and I had to pause after every length or so and yank it back into place.

"Okay, everyone! Let's go!" Dale motioned for us to get out of the pool and line up at the starting blocks. I climbed out, shook my shoulders and arms to loosen up, and did a few quick stretches.

Ross threw me a wink. "Gonna beatcha," he said.

"Keep dreaming," I countered. Joanne tapped me on the shoulder.

"Dale says Beth's the anchor, and you're supposed to lead off, so we'll let Lisa go second, okay? She's a little faster than me."

"Sure," I said.

"Girls 4 by 100 freestyle relay, get ready," Dale shouted from the side of the pool. The four relay teams crowded up to the starting blocks.

I gave my arms one last shake, tugged at my bathing suit, and stepped up on the starting block. I snapped my goggles over my eyes and pressed them carefully to make sure they wouldn't leak.

Everything suddenly grew silent, just the way it did in a real competition. The whole team watched intently. I could feel their stares behind me, and I took a deep breath and looked out across the pool.

"Take your marks!" Dale yelled.

I bent over and grasped the end of the starting block with my hands, my chest resting against my thighs, my toes curled around the edge for an extra push when I dove.

Then something horrible happened. My swimsuit began to creep upwards — very, very fast. I knew that in about two seconds the whole swim team would get a terrific view of my exposed rear end.

Sweat stood out on my forehead. If a swimmer moves at all, even their hands, after the announcer has said, "take your marks," it counts as a false start. But this wasn't a real competition, and anyway, I didn't care. I let go of the starting block, just as Dale yelled:

"GO!"

I was so startled I lost my balance, teetered and wiggled and flapped my arms for what seemed like a year, before I bellyflopped into the pool with a gigantic splash.

I surfaced to the sound of uncontrollable giggles and raucous yells. Even Dale was leaning helplessly against the flag pole, laughing.

"Hey Josie, nice form!" Ross whooped from the edge. "Where can I learn to dive like that?"

My whole face felt like fire. I wished there was something I could say so I wouldn't feel like such an idiot, but humiliation choked me. Instead, I climbed out of the pool and just stood there, dripping.

Joanne and Beth were leaning against each other, shrieking with laughter. "I've ... I've never seen anything so funny in my life," gasped Beth. "The way you fell, Josie — you looked like an ostrich trying to fly."

"Okay, you guys. Let's try to settle down," Dale said, but his words were useless, since he still wore a giant grin. Even when he tried to look serious, that grin stuck there.

I tried to smile and pretend that I thought my bellyflop was funny, but the attempt was a failure. The most I could manage was a sickly grimace.

"All right, everyone." This time Dale managed to command attention. "We can all thank Josie later for providing comic relief, but let's get back to practice, okay? Let's start off the boys 4 by 100 freestyle relay."

While Dale marshalled everyone into order, I lingered behind. Why did I always manage to mess up, just when I wanted to do well? I felt discouraged, as well as embarrassed. But I also felt an overwhelming urge to wring Melissa's neck. This was all her fault, after all. If she hadn't messed up my stuff …

I clenched my jaw. There was absolutely no way I was going to let her get away with this.

6

My Sister the Slug

Melissa!" I stormed into the house. "Get down here right this minute!"

"I can't. I'm doing my nails." The voice floated faintly down from Melissa's bedroom.

I stomped up the stairs and burst into her room. "You … you … you are such a …" I sputtered, unable to think of anything bad enough to say.

"Terrific person?" Melissa suggested, blowing gingerly on her wet, pink-tipped fingernails, as she lounged on her bed.

"Such a total slug!" I said. The insult wasn't great, but it would do.

"Oh." Melissa waved her fingertips with a complete lack of concern. "Why?"

"Because you shrank my team suit, that's why," I yelled. "I've told you forty million times how to wash my swimsuits, or else to just leave them for me to do, but no! You have to go and wreck them. And today, because of you, I totally humiliated myself in front of the whole swim club."

"Really? What happened?" Melissa asked with interest, sitting up.

I found myself telling her the whole story. I'm not sure why it all came spilling out. Maybe it was because my pride was so bruised with the memory of all the swimmers laughing so hard that they could barely stand up. Or maybe it was car-pooling home with Ross. He and three other guys from the team didn't stop teasing me the whole way home. It was the longest car ride of my life.

Call it temporary insanity, trying to talk to Melissa. Because when I was finished, she laughed.

"Don't laugh at me!" I hollered, my voice finally breaking. All the embarrassment and dejection I'd been holding back came bursting out. "It isn't funny."

Melissa tried to stifle a giggle and look sympathetic, but it was too late. I swung around and rushed to my room, flopping face-down on my bed — sneakers, jacket, swim bag and all.

"It's not fair!" I thought. "If it weren't for my stupid sister, my life would be just fine." I kicked my feet into the quilt, as if pounding it would erase all the humiliation I felt about the afternoon, and all the frustration I felt about putting up with Melissa the Perfect.

It wasn't long before lying with my nose squished into my pillow and my jacket twisted around me was very uncomfortable. I sat up and sighed. I'm not the type to sit around snivelling, anyway. I'd rather do something about a problem — it's just that there didn't seem to be any way to fix my problems with Melissa, short of getting her a one-way ticket to northern Mongolia.

"Well, then," I said to myself. "Forget about it. Melissa's a permanent pain in the butt, and you made a complete idiot out of yourself today. So what?"

I said it as convincingly as possible and waited a few minutes until I felt calmer. Then I reached into my swim bag and pulled out the information sheet from Dale, kicked off my sneakers, and dropped my jacket on the floor. I could hear Melissa's radio, so I went back to her room and stuck my head around the door.

"Where's Mom and Dad?" I asked stiffly.

"Getting Chinese take-out," Melissa said. "They should be back right away."

"Okay." I went downstairs and began pulling plates from the cupboard. By the time I'd finished setting the table, Mom and Dad were coming through the back door, loaded down with delicious smelling cartons and two big bottles of pop.

"A treat tonight," Dad said, ruffling my hair. But I noticed that his smile looked tired, and I wished I didn't have to hand him that information sheet with its expensive total.

"No pop for you, Josie," Mom said. "Not until you have some milk. Have to keep your championship strength up."

I grinned and reached for the milk carton. Melissa came downstairs and plunked herself in a chair, just in time to be handed a plateful of rice, sweet-and-sour chicken, ginger beef, and mixed vegetables.

"Mmmm," she said, digging in with gusto. "Smells great."

"Yeah," I said, resenting her timing. She never had to help do anything, it seemed. "But you get to clean up after. I set the table."

Melissa wrinkled her nose.

"Let's talk about that later," Mom said hastily. "We have something else we need to discuss."

"Before we do," I said, "I need to give you this." I passed her the information sheet. "Dale made us promise not to forget to give it to our parents right away."

Mom took the paper and began to read. Her eyes widened and her mouth drew down into a frown. Creases crept up her forehead and she silently handed it to my father.

Dad's face grew more tired as he read it. I cast a frightened glance at Melissa, but she was too absorbed in her Chinese food to notice anything else.

"What is it, Mom?" I finally asked.

Dad laid the paper down on the table and faced us. "There's something you girls need to know. I've been laid off."

I swallowed. Melissa looked up, her mouth full.

"What does that mean?" I asked.

Melissa chomped on a piece of broccoli. "It means Dad's out of work, dummy."

I glared at her. Dad winced.

"I wouldn't exactly put it that way," he said.

"Will you get your job back?" I asked.

"Probably not," Dad said. "The company is downsizing, and they don't plan to replace any employees for a while, if ever. But I might get some contract work with them, and that would help."

"What your dad means," Mom interjected, "is that he can do some freelance-type stuff for a while, until something full-time comes along, but meanwhile we all have to cut back on any unnecessary spending since my job will have to cover all the bills." She looked pointedly at Melissa and me. "Okay?"

We nodded. Melissa didn't look bothered. After all, she had a flyer route, which earned her extra money for things she wanted, and none of her activities cost a lot of money. Melissa played the clarinet in the school band and was a member of the school soccer and basketball teams and the art club. Compared to what Dad had to spend on my swim program, Melissa was cheap.

But what if Mom and Dad decide they can't afford to pay for swimming this year, I worried. Suppose they think it's an unnecessary expenditure? I looked at my parents, searching their faces. They looked sad, helpless — even defeated. And then I knew. We couldn't afford the swim program. They were going to tell me I had to quit.

Suddenly the Chinese food turned to a lump in my stomach, and I felt sick.

"May I be excused?" I muttered, shoving my chair back. I didn't wait for an answer but ran upstairs and threw myself on my bed for the second time that day.

This was the worst day of my entire life. I buried my face in my pillow, and this time I *really* cried.

7

The Biggest Effort Yet

"Wow, that's tough," Delaney said. She shoved her jacket into her locker and pulled out her math text. "Are you sure?"

"Well, they never actually said so, but I know that's what's going to happen," I said as we walked down the hall. I'd just finished telling Delaney about the night before. "I mean, when they said unnecessary spending, what else could they mean?"

"I don't know, Josie. Your parents are pretty great. I think maybe you should talk to them about all this."

I shook my head. "No way. If they don't think swimming is important, then I'm not going to let them see how much it means to me."

"I think you're wrong. If they didn't think swimming was important, why would they get up at five in the morning to drive you to practice and stuff? If I had to get up at five almost every morning, I'd just about die," she joked.

"Well, anyway, I'm not quitting the team, no matter what," I said firmly. "The team offers one scholarship every year to a swimmer. I've never applied, because you have to need the money and show the most potential. But I'm going to talk to Dale about it tonight. I think they award it soon."

"Do you think you could win it?" Delaney asked.

"I have to," I said grimly. "I have no choice."

"That's a lot to do," Delaney commented. "Win a scholarship and a science fair by the end of next week."

I clapped a hand to my forehead. "The science fair! I forgot all about it."

"You forgot?" Delaney said. "You were supposed to look up topics for a project two days ago."

"I know. I'm sorry. I'll do it tonight, I promise. It's just that with this big crisis, I haven't been able to concentrate."

"At least you have an excuse," Delaney said, dodging into her math classroom. I made a face at her and she laughed. "We have to get started, so let's work in the library at lunch, okay?"

"Okay."

The morning passed slowly. In science class, Mr. P. asked Delaney and me what our project for the science fair was going to be, and I had to tell him that we hadn't decided on anything yet. He looked disappointed, but I told him we'd get started right away, and he offered to help us come up with something. For a minute I was tempted, but then I remembered how he'd compared me to Melissa. I wanted this project to be my very own — mine and Delaney's. I wanted to prove that I was just as smart as Melissa, and I couldn't do that with her old teacher hanging over my shoulder.

So I told him politely, no thanks, and went with Delaney to the library.

Half an hour later we looked at each other helplessly. The neatly stacked shelves of books surrounding us were a sad contrast to the muddled mess of reference materials and magazines heaped on our table.

"Well, what now?" she asked, thumping the last encyclopedia closed. "You've said no to every idea I've come up with."

"No offence, Dee, but I really wanted something spectacular. Doing a science project on plant cells or toxic waste just sounds too … well, boring. We won't get noticed with an entry like that."

Delaney grimaced. "Josie, the science fair is next week. We don't have time to do nuclear physics here."

"I know," I said. "I just want to do something that'll really blow the socks off the judges, and Melissa."

"Well, like what?" Delaney said.

"We could build an engine and show how it works," I suggested.

Delaney made a face. "I'm no mechanic. I have no idea how to do that, and anyway, where would we find stuff to build an engine?"

"How about an atomic bomb?" I said.

"Build one?" Delaney snorted. "Very funny."

"No, just do a project on how they work."

"Nathan Jovovich is already doing that."

"Oh." I rested my chin in my hands. "Well …"

"We could do charts on nutrition," Delaney said. "How certain foods affect your body and all that."

I wrinkled my nose. "Yuck. I'd rather do a report on garbage."

"Well, excuuuse me," Delaney huffed.

"How about a volcano or something?" I suggested. "We could make it erupt."

"Oh, that's original. Someone's done a volcano in every science fair since grade one."

"Yeah, but ours could be really different. We could make it huge and put a lightbulb inside so the lava would glow in the dark." I was starting to get excited about the idea. "Wouldn't that be great?"

Delaney considered. "Well, it would look pretty cool if it glowed in the dark. We could turn the lights off in the gym when it's our turn to be judged."

"And then everyone would have to watch our entry!" I crowed. "Delaney, that's perfect."

"We'll still have to do some maps and charts and stuff, though," Delaney said. "The judges will want to see some research."

I brushed that worry aside. "No problem."

Delaney shook her head. "Okay, but just remember, if anything goes wrong, this was all your idea."

"Deal."

***

Mr. P. approved our project idea, so that night my room was a wilderness of scattered reference books, crumpled notepaper, coloured felt pens, poster boards, and a giant economy-size bag of potato chips. I was lying on my stomach, painstakingly drawing a map showing where some of the most famous volcanoes were located, when someone tapped on my door.

"C'mon in," I called.

Delaney peeked in. "Your lips are purple," she said. "And your chin has orange dots."

I touched my lips with a fingertip. "Rats. It's the felt pens. I keep tapping them against my mouth when I'm thinking."

"Yuck." Delaney surveyed the room. "What a mess!"

"It's a creative scientific process," I retorted. "Look what I've done so far." I held up the map and the partial report I'd written.

"Wow." Delaney took the report and scanned it. "You must've worked like a maniac to get this much done."

"Yeah. Did you bring your sleeping bag?"

Delaney gave me a puzzled look. "No. Why?"

"Because you're going to be here 'til at least midnight. I guess you'll have to make do with a pillow on the floor."

She tossed a potato chip at me. "This isn't supposed to be a NASA experiment. The teachers don't expect you to be a genius."

"Yeah, right. You aren't Melissa-the-Einstein-Brain's little sister."

"It's not that bad," Delaney said.

"Oh, yes, it is," I answered. I pointed to the pile of newspapers beside my desk. "I've got most of the stuff for the papier mâché. We should get started on our volcano tonight."

"Okay." Delaney began to untangle the coat hangers she'd brought to use inside the volcano and pulled several tubes of acrylic paint from her coat pocket. "You know, you've done an amazing amount of work. At this rate, you'll pull your science grade up to an A+."

"That would be great," I said, colouring in a bar graph with green felt. "Except that I skipped swim practice to get all this done."

Delaney stared at me in amazement. "You skipped swim practice? I don't believe it. Why?"

I shrugged. "I guess this is important to me. Besides, I'll go tomorrow."

"I thought you were going to ask Dale about the scholarship today."

"I was. I'll ask him tomorrow."

"You're scared, aren't you? You're scared you won't get it, and you don't want to find out."

I swallowed. Sometimes it seemed as though my thoughts must be printed on my forehead, the way Delaney could read my mind.

"Yeah, sort of," I admitted. "We were supposed to apply weeks ago. But it's my last chance! If I don't get it, I don't know what I'll do."

"Well, that was really dumb, if you ask me. The longer you wait, the more likely it is that Dale will give the scholarship to someone else."

"Thanks a lot."

"Well, it's true."

"I know. I'll talk to him tomorrow, I promise. Now can we get back to work?"

Delaney saluted. "Yes, ma'am," she said.

We laughed, grabbed some potato chips, and settled down to work on the greatest science project in Waterson family history.

8

A Fighting Chance

I chewed nervously on my bottom lip and hesitated in the cold outside the big glass doors that opened into the pool lobby. I'd hurried to my after-school practice so I'd have time to talk to Dale about the scholarship fund, but every joint in my body seemed to have turned into soggy spaghetti, and I found it hard to move.

I could either confront Dale, or freeze out here in the cold autumn wind. I exhaled slowly and reached for the door handle.

Dale's office was empty. I had to search for him and finally found him on the pool deck retying new elastic tubing in the hand paddles.

"Hi Josie," he said cheerfully. "How come you're here so early?"

"I needed to talk to you," I answered, wriggling out of my coat. Now I was starting to swelter from the steamy warmth of the pool.

"About what?" Dale concentrated on tying a knot near the end of the thick tubing.

"Um ..." I hesitated, then blurted in a rush, "It's about the scholarship. I was wondering if it was too late to apply."

Dale looked up with concern. "Why, Josie? Is something wrong?"

"Sort of." I stared at my sneakers. "My fees are a lot higher this year, and my dad just got laid off from work. My parents said we have to watch extra spending."

"Does that mean they want you to quit?"

I nodded. "I think so."

"But your parents have always been really supportive of your swim program, Josie. And we do a lot of fund-raising that will lower the cost for you. Have you talked to your mom and dad about it?" Dale asked.

"Not exactly."

"Why not?"

I squirmed. "I didn't want them to tell me I had to quit."

Dale nodded slowly. "I can understand that. But talking to them would at least let you know where you stand, right?"

"Yeah, I guess so," I said. "But what about the scholarship, Dale? If I won that, then I wouldn't have to worry about whether or not my parents could afford the fees, or wanted to help with fund-raising, right?"

A pained expression crossed his face. "Josie," he said.

I knew right then he was about to tell me precisely the news that I didn't want to hear.

"I'm sorry, but Beth's got the scholarship. She applied a month ago, and we decided last week."

"Oh." I studied a chipped tile in the floor and tried to control the flush rising in my face. "Well, that's okay. I kind of figured maybe it was too late."

"Josie, talk to your mom and dad." Dale placed a hand on my shoulder. "Maybe it's not as bad as you think."

"Yeah," I said, turning away. "Thanks anyway." I trudged to the locker room and began to get changed. Absolutely the last thing I felt like doing was getting into that pool and practising, but if my place on the swim team was about to be terminated, I figured I'd better make the most of whatever time I had left.

I heard the locker-room door open and looked up, expecting to see Lisa or Joanne, or another friend from the team. Instead I saw Melissa, a nylon gym bag over one shoulder, holding a photocopied pamphlet with the swim team logo blazoned on the front.

I stared at her in shock. Melissa gave me a friendly smile and sat down on the wooden bench in front of the lockers.

"Hi," she said.

"What are you doing here?" I said.

Melissa waved the pamphlet. "I'm thinking about joining the non-competitive program. Dale says it's really good, and I thought it would be fun."

Fun? The word sizzled deep inside me, and a scorching hot anger began to fill my chest.

"Fun?" I said flatly.

"Yeah. Mom said I could use my flyer-route money if I wanted to join. Dale sounds like a terrific coach."

Dale. My coach. Melissa had been talking to my coach. The thoughts flew wildly in my brain. Again. She was doing it again. Everything I had, everything I was good at she wanted to strip from me. Everything. Teachers, friends, Mom and Dad's attention, school. Even swimming, the only thing I had left. Now I didn't even have that, and Melissa wanted to take my place.

The anger rose higher and seemed to choke me. I stepped over to Melissa and snatched the pamphlet out of her hand. I tore it up, ripping it smaller and smaller, while Melissa watched, open mouthed. Then I threw the pieces to the ground. They floated like confetti, but as they sank onto the wet tiles I ground my heel into as many as I could reach, until the floor was covered with bits of soggy paper.

Melissa recovered her power of speech at last. "What did you do that for?" she demanded.

"Go away." I glared at her. "I don't want you on my team."

"No!" Melissa's face was red, and she tossed her hair defiantly. "I have as much right to be here as you do. You're acting like a spoiled brat."

I stood still. My breathing sounded loud in my ears, and I felt like I couldn't stand one more horrible minute with my sister. I whirled around, yanked my jeans and jacket over my swimsuit, shoved my sockless feet into my sneakers, and grabbed my swim bag. I ran out of the locker room before Melissa could say another word.

The wind whipped at my hair, and my sneakers slapped against the sidewalk. I ran until I was out of breath and had a pain in my side. I slowed to a walk.

I would not cry. I was determined not to cry. It was just that everything was so awful. Why did things seem to work out perfectly for people like Melissa? And why did they fall totally apart for people like me, no matter how hard I tried?

I gritted my teeth against the flood of tears that threatened to overflow. I tried hard, but I lost the battle. I sat down on the sidewalk curb several blocks from the community centre and watched my tears dot the concrete like raindrops.

9

Back to the Starting Block

Swoosh! Swoosh! Swoosh! My arms cut into the water like swords, but the anger I felt just wouldn't diminish.

Last night had been a disaster. I refused to speak to Melissa, and she clearly wasn't interested in talking to me. Breakfast wasn't much better, and it had been a relief to escape to school.

Now at swim practice, I was more ticked off than ever. Melissa had shown up for the non-competitive team, and even though they practised in the lanes for slower swimmers, and I was in the fast lane, I still couldn't help noticing all the attention she attracted. Ross was already teasing her, and Dale seemed happy to spend time with her, explaining how warm-ups and workouts were done, instead of helping me improve my 200-metre butterfly time for the upcoming meet.

I hadn't told him that I would be quitting yet. I wanted one last day of swimming the way I always had. So as far as Dale knew, I was still in the running for a medal at the 200 butterfly. And I definitely considered preparing for a competition more important than explaining how many lengths are in a 400-metre warm-up to dopey Melissa.

I blew a wrathful stream of bubbles into the water and thrust my head up for another breath. *Swoosh! Swoosh! Swoosh!* I kicked powerfully toward the edge of the pool, ripped off my goggles, and squinted up at the clock.

Yes! I threw my fist in the air. I'd cut two whole seconds off my time for 200 fly, and that was without diving from the starting block, or wearing a racing suit. I was improving for sure. A surge of adrenalin pumped through me, and I looked for Dale to share the good news.

He was watching Melissa with a thoughtful look on his face. She was doing freestyle. It looked kind of sloppy to me, but Dale seemed interested. I climbed out of the pool and hurried over to him.

"Dale, guess what!" I tugged on the sleeve of his sweatshirt, hoping to get his complete attention.

"What, Josie?" Dale turned toward me, but his eyes were still on the pool.

"Dale, listen!" I said. "I just took two whole seconds off my 200-metre butterfly. And I didn't even start with a dive. Isn't that great?"

Dale finally looked me in the eye. "Josie, that's terrific!" he said.

I felt warm all through.

"You've really been working hard, kiddo. I saw you plowing through the water over there," said Dale. "That's what it takes — good, tough effort. I'm proud of you."

I glowed.

"In fact, if your sister Melissa has your kind of dedication, we might have two Waterson champions." Dale's voice was enthusiastic.

The glow died.

"She needs a lot of training, of course," Dale said, pointing to Melissa. "See how she doesn't get enough power on her arm stroke? But still, Josie, she's got some great potential. She's tall and her upper body is strong. Someday we might have a 400-metre freestyler here."

"Oh. That's great," I said flatly.

The realization that I wouldn't be here tomorrow, but that Melissa would, suddenly hit me so hard I could scarcely breathe. Melissa really would take my place. I realized that deep inside I'd been secretly hoping Melissa would be a huge flop in the pool. Instead, like always, she impressed everyone, including Dale.

I swallowed. "Well, I guess I'll finish the workout," I said slowly.

Dale clapped me on the shoulder. "Keep up the good work, Josie."

The wonderful feeling of accomplishment I'd felt only a moment before had completely faded, leaving me sagging and empty. I slid back into the pool and began the rest of the sets.

Even though I tried to work hard, my body no longer co-operated. I swam three more sets of 200-metre butterfly, and not once did I come close to equalling my time on the first one.

I finished the rest of the workout mechanically and crawled out of the pool. Melissa brushed past, deliberately ignoring me, her lips set in a stubborn frown.

I dangled my legs over the edge of the pool, waiting for Melissa to shower and leave the locker room. I didn't want to face her.

I didn't feel as angry. Now I just felt like a bottle of pop that had lost its fizzle — flat and lifeless.

"Everything okay, Josie?" Dale asked, as he pushed the giant spool for the lane ropes back toward the wall. The pool time was scheduled now for public swimming, and a few women in flowered bathing suits were getting into the water and jogging with empty bleach bottles.

I watched them push the bottles back and forth as they jogged and talked.

"Yeah," I said finally. "Everything's just fine."

10

The Science Fair

On the day of the science fair, the junior-high gym was teeming with kids. It was like being in the middle of an anthill, and somehow Delaney and I had to get ourselves and all our stuff in there to set up our project.

"Wow, this must be the biggest science fair ever," Delaney said, watching wide-eyed as a couple of boys rigged up a glass aquarium for what looked like two dozen lively frogs. "I've never seen this many kids enter before."

"Did someone offer big prize money?" I joked glumly. "Maybe we'll win it. I sure could use it."

Delaney shifted her poster boards and squeezed my hand. I'd told her about how I didn't get the scholarship and how Melissa had suddenly shown an interest in joining the team. Her sympathy helped, but it didn't change anything for me. I still felt depressed.

That's why I had spent the night before developing our secret weapon, guaranteed to win us first prize. I hadn't told Delaney about it yet, mostly because I knew she'd tell me I was crazy, but I was sure my idea was absolutely terrific.

Originally, Delaney and I had planned to use a lightbulb inside the volcano to light up the painted red streaks on the volcano's sides and the bright red tip of the crater. We'd made the papier mâché thicker near the bottom of the volcano, so the light wouldn't show through, and we'd painted it with grey and black paint so everything would look as realistic as possible. To make the volcano erupt, Delaney had planned to use her mother's pump-style plant sprayer filled with red paint. Her idea was to cut a hole in the back wall of the volcano and gently squirt the paint up and out of the crater. It was a good idea, but mine was better. I couldn't wait to get started.

Mr. P. saw us wandering around and helped us find our booth. He also helped us carry in our volcano, which was mounted on a square piece of plywood and weighed about a ton. Delaney began unstacking the posters and arranging them on the cardboard divider behind our booth, while I began setting up the table for the volcano.

"What are you doing?" Delaney asked, when she saw me pull out three large candles, a squat, wide-mouthed jar filled with gooey red stuff, and a wire stand I'd made out of coat-hangers. "What are these for?"

"These," I whispered, "are going to help us win this science fair."

Delaney gave me a suspicious look. "Josie, is this another one of your crazy ideas?"

"It's not crazy," I said. "It's going to be fanatastic. See, look."

I carefully lifted the volcano off the plywood and placed the candles in the centre. I fixed the wire stand over top of them and made sure everything was sturdy before I picked up the jar and shook the contents. "The candles are just the right height to heat the bottom of the jar, once I set it in the stand," I said. "The light from the candles will still make the volcano glow in the dark, but they'll also heat up the liquid in the jar, and it'll bubble over, just like a real volcano. Cool, huh?"

Delaney shook her head. "I don't know, Josie. Did you try this out already?"

"Yeah, last night. I only used one candle, and I didn't put it in the volcano, because I didn't want to get it all messed up, but it worked just fine."

Delaney picked up the jar. "Yuck. What *is* this stuff?"

"Water and cornstarch cooked together with red food colouring."

"It looks disgusting."

"It makes great lava," I said, taking the jar from her and unscrewing the lid. I set it carefully on the wire stand directly over the candles and replaced the volcano, so it covered the whole thing. "Now all we have to do is light the candles and turn off the lights," I said.

"How are you going to light them?" Delaney asked.

"I'll use these long matchsticks," I said, holding up one of the several I'd swiped from our fireplace at home. "I'll just push the lighted match through the hole we made in the back of the volcano."

Delaney shrugged. "Okay. But remember what I said. If anything goes wrong —"

"Yeah, yeah, I know. It was all my idea. You'll wish you hadn't said that when we win and I get to take all the credit," I said.

Mr. P. strolled by and looked pleased when he saw our completed project. "You've done a nice job, girls," he said. "I'm really impressed."

I braced myself for some remark about how Melissa's seventh-grade project was even better, but none came. Mr. P. just smiled and said, "Good job, Josie. I knew there was a budding scientist in there somewhere."

I couldn't help grinning. Now, if only we could win! Then that would prove I could be just as smart as Melissa, and maybe my parents would stop thinking of her as the star genius in our family.

"Okay, girls." Mr. P. glanced at his watch. "Judging starts in about half an hour. You have time to wander around and look at the other entries, if you like."

"Sure," Delaney said eagerly. "Want to, Josie?"

I nodded. The two of us walked around the gym, pointing out the exhibits we liked the best. Delaney thought the one on marine biology was neat because the eighth-graders who did it brought a big fish tank with papier mâché models of different kinds of sea life in it. I liked the project on the rainforests, with its colourful reports on the mysterious plants and insects that lived in them.

Melissa's entry was with the rest of the ninth-grade projects. I hated to admit it, but it was good. She'd done a project on electricity and had rigged up a bunch of gadgets to demonstrate how it works.

I didn't go up too close. I didn't want to talk to her, and I hoped she didn't see me. Besides, it was almost time for the judging, and Delaney and I hurried back to our booth.

Everything was ready.

I began retacking some of the posters and fussing about the best angle to show off the volcano.

"Josie, it looks fine," Delaney protested.

"I just want everything to be perfect," I said.

With shaking hands I inserted the matchstick, its small flame burning brightly as I poked it toward the candles. Each wick lit easily and the candles burned hotly just underneath the jar on the wire stand. I breathed a sigh of relief. Everything seemed to be working smoothly. The lava mixture would be hot enough by the time the judges came to our entry to bubble over impressively, and all that would be left to do was pick up our first-prize ribbon.

Pffftt to you, Melissa, I thought, mentally sticking out my tongue. I did create a great science fair entry after all.

Delaney peered inside the volcano through the matchstick hole. "Don't you think those candles should be more in the centre?" she asked. "That one is kind of close to the side of the volcano."

"I couldn't get them much closer," I said. "The wire stand is in the way." I elbowed her aside and looked for myself. "I think they'll be okay."

Delaney shrugged doubtfully but said nothing more.

I mentally rehearsed what I wanted to say when the judges presented themselves at our booth. I straightened the maps, smoothed down the front of my shirt and brushed my hair back from my face.

"How do I look?" I asked anxiously.

"Fine," Delaney said, rolling her eyes. I ignored her and watched nervously as the judges strolled up to our table.

"Well, what have we here?" asked the first judge, who was Mr. Wentworth, the assistant principal.

Mr. Wentworth was a strict, dour-looking teacher with a balding head that shone under the gym's lights. His ample stomach and chest had been tightly stuffed into his grey suit, and I hoped the buttons would hold. From the pressure on them, if they popped, they'd become instant projectile missiles. Somebody could get hurt.

I smiled. "We've done a project on volcanoes, sir."

"Hmmm." Mr. Wentworth glanced at the colourful maps, briefly inspected our volcano model and made a few notes on his clipboard. "Very nice," he said, preparing to walk away. The other two judges had looked on with polite interest, but no one made an attempt to ask us any more questions.

"Wait!" I called. The judges stopped. "You haven't seen our demonstration yet. Our volcano really works. It'll just take a few more minutes for the lava to get hot." My knees quaked with nervousness, but I just couldn't let the judges leave without showing off my brilliant idea.

"All right, then." Mr. Wentworth looked at his watch. "We can wait a few minutes. Let's see what you have."

Eagerly I showed off the various parts of the volcano that we'd painstakingly painted on the surface — the grey ash, the black lava rock, and the red molten lava that appeared to be flowing down from the crater. By then I could hear the unmistakable hissing and popping of the hot lava mixture getting ready to boil over.

"Go turn off the lights, Dee," I whispered. Delaney ran and flicked off the gym lights, leaving everyone in a dim gloom, illuminated only by the few high windows and emergency lights.

The chattering and rustling in the gym slowly stopped. Everyone was wondering, of course, why the lights had been turned off, and all eyes focused on me, Delaney, and our volcano.

The red crater glowed eerily, and the thick-sounding sputters of the lava grew louder. The flames from the candles not only lit the red painted streaks along the volcano walls, but shone through the glass jar and its goopy, translucent contents, making the inside of the crater look like a real bubbling volcano.

I grinned in triumph. The lava mixture started to bubble high enough to overflow a little, and it began to ooze slowly down the sides of the volcano.

Mr. Wentworth looked impressed. "Very realistic. Look, there's even smoke rising from the crater."

I smiled and nodded. "Yes. We worked very hard on building —" I stopped. Smoke? A thin line of white smoke was curling up from the edges of the crater. I stepped forward and looked in horror as a black patch on the volcano wall grew blacker and was swallowed by a growing orange flame.

"Help!" I panicked. "Fire! It's on fire!" Without thinking I leaped from behind our booth and dashed for the fire extinguisher on the wall. Delaney puffed and blew, trying to blow out the flame.

"Don't!" I cried. "You'll only make it worse!"

Mr. P. heard the commotion and came hurrying to help. I nearly collided with him as I raced back with the fire extinguisher and fumbled with the clasp.

"No, Josie, it's okay. We've got it out." Delaney waved the last of the smoke away from her face and Mr. Wentworth stepped back from the table, where he'd helped Delaney smother the flame.

I looked dismally at the wreckage as the gym lights were flicked back on, and a slow, fiery-hot blush crept up my neck and burned my cheeks. Everyone was staring, open mouthed. If ever a person could really sink through the floor and disappear, I prayed it would be me.

"Well, girls, nice try," Mr. Wentworth said. "It was an interesting exhibit, but next time check for fire hazards, all right?"

I nodded glumly.

As the judges progressed on to other entries, the students turned their attention back to the science fair, but I could still hear snickers and whispers throughout the gym.

Mr. P., who had remained silent as I began to clean up the booth, stepped forward.

"Josie."

I turned around slowly.

"You girls told me you were going to use a lightbulb when I approved this project idea. We never discussed candles, or fake lava that boiled over."

I squirmed and looked at Delaney. "I know," I said. "This … this was all my idea. I, um, guess I didn't think it through enough."

"No. And neither did you check with me. Mr. Wentworth will probably have a few choice words to say to me on that subject later," Mr. P. said.

"I'm sorry Mr. P.," I gulped. "I just wanted our project to be spectacular."

"Well, let's put it this way. No one will forget it, that's for sure," Mr. P. said. He grinned suddenly. "All right, let's get this mess cleaned up." He went off in search of paper towels and a garbage can.

Delaney began untacking the blackened posters.

"I'm really sorry, Dee. I didn't mean to wreck everything," I whispered.

"I know." Delaney shrugged. "But if I'd known what you were planning to do, I would've brought some marshmallows."

"Marshmallows? What for?"

"To toast over the fire." Delaney snickered as I swatted her with a map.

11

Me and Melissa

"Why me?" I moaned. I was crumpled up on the floor of my bedroom, completely dejected. It was a relief that Delaney wasn't angry with me for completely messing up our chances to win a prize at the science fair, but I was angry at myself. I'd loused up the one chance I had to prove to my parents that I was as smart as Melissa. And even worse, Melissa had seen the disaster.

Delaney handed me a tissue. "Blow your nose."

"I haven't been crying," I said.

"I know. But you must have been crying inside, because your nose is all stuffed up. Blow."

I blew. "I can't believe that happened."

"I can. Stuff like that just happens to you, Josie. You're like an accident magnet."

"Thanks a lot."

Delaney plopped down beside me. "The bubbling lava was a good idea, though. I was pretty impressed until you flubbed it."

"Is that supposed to make me feel better?"

"Well, sort of."

"Dee, my whole life is a shambles. I lost my chance at the swimming scholarship, I have no money, I'm practically failing science, and now I've gone and humiliated myself in front of the assistant principal, not to mention almost the entire school. I will never live this down!"

"Well, I doubt Mr. Wentworth will ever forget you, that's for sure."

"Dee, if you can't say anything to cheer me up, be quiet, will you?" I said wearily. "This has got to be the worst thing that's ever happened to me."

"How about the time in second grade, when you came down with the chicken pox and didn't know it until we had already left for the field trip to the Tyrell Museum in Drumheller? Remember, they had to cancel the trip and turn the bus around to bring you home, and even then half the class caught chicken pox anyway. All the kids were so mad."

"This is worse than that."

"Well, what about in fourth grade, when you held that burping contest with Jimmy Brader, and the teacher was right behind you when you let go with the biggest burp anyone ever heard? Everyone in the cafeteria laughed for days."

"This is way worse than that."

"Well, there was that time in grade five when you —"

"Look, Dee," I interrupted. "I appreciate you trying to take my mind off my latest disaster by reminding me of all the dumb things I've ever done in my life, but I'd really rather not talk about them right now, okay?" I stared up at the ceiling. "My life is technically over, and I'd like to enjoy what's left without any extra misery."

Delaney looked at me and shrugged. "Okay. But I don't think this mess is that bad. The chicken pox thing was worse, and you survived. I have to go anyway. My mom wants me to practise my piano lesson before dinner. I'll call you after, okay?"

"Okay." I didn't move from the floor. Delaney let herself out, and I continued to stare up at the ceiling. I deliberately avoided looking at my poster. I hadn't been able to bring myself to take it down yet, but I would. Soon. There was no point in having it up, since my swimming dreams, along with everything else, had virtually been flushed down the toilet. I thought about the upcoming swim meet — how hard I'd been training, and how Dale had thought I could win. That hurt, and I quickly pushed those thoughts out of my mind.

I was becoming interested in the different pictures I could pick out in the stipple patterns on the ceiling when Melissa knocked softly on the bedroom door. "Jo? Can I come in?"

I didn't move. "Yeah. I guess so." My hands were propped behind my head, and I didn't bother to look at her when she came in.

Melissa sat on my bed and regarded me silently. When I didn't say anything, she finally spoke.

"I saw what happened today."

"Yeah. Who didn't?"

"If it's any comfort, most of the kids thought it was pretty funny."

"It's not. Much comfort, I mean. I completely destroyed my chances of winning the science fair. They gave the grade-seven award to those nerds beside us who did a project on plant cells."

"That doesn't matter, Josie. At least you tried. And Mr. P. will give you a good grade for it. He's a really great teacher."

"I bet you won," I said. I hadn't stayed around to find out who the eighth and ninth-grade winners were.

"Nope. I got an honourable mention, though."

"Honourable mention? That's it?" I looked at her. That was the worst placing Melissa had ever had. "Don't you care?"

"Not really. I did a project on what I was interested in. If I wanted to win, I would have done one on a topic that I knew the judges would love. Winning's not that important."

"Hah. That from Miss Straight-A Genius."

Melissa was silent. Then she said something that startled me. "Josie, do you think that I'm just smart, and that's why I get good grades?"

"Yeah. You're lucky."

"No, you're wrong. I have to work hard to do well. Really hard."

I snorted.

"I do, too. I'm not a super-brain like you think I am. I spend hours doing homework, just like you spend hours in the pool. That's why I get such good marks and why you're so good at swimming."

I blew a weary sigh. I didn't feel like fighting with Melissa. Any other time I might actually appreciate her admitting that she wasn't perfect, but my worries about having to quit the swim team overshadowed everything, including the science fair disaster. So I told her that.

"Actually, that's what I came in here to talk to you about," Melissa said.

Oh, great.

"Delaney told me you didn't get the scholarship," she said quietly. I was surprised by the sympathy in her voice.

I swallowed. "Yeah, well. I guess Beth needed it more. And anyway, she applied for it ages ago. I asked at the last minute. Maybe they figured I didn't really need the money."

"Yeah, but you really deserved it," Melissa said.

I tilted my head to look at her, but there wasn't a glimmer of a smile on her face. She really meant it. "Thanks," I said.

Neither of us spoke for a moment.

"Do you think Mom and Dad will make you quit?" Melissa asked hesitantly.

"Probably." I didn't even feel angry any more. Just empty.

"Listen, Jo," Melissa said, her words coming out in a rush. "I know the swim team is really important to you, and — if you want — I'd like to … um, help you pay for it. With my flyer-route money."

I sat up. "What do you mean?"

"I could quit the team. I was just swimming for fun anyway. It's not like it is for you."

"You'd really do that?" I asked incredulously.

Melissa looked uncomfortable. "Yeah."

"Why?"

"Josie, you're my sister!" Melissa exclaimed. "I'm really proud of you. Why do you think I joined the swim team in the first place?" She didn't stop to let me answer. "Because you made it sound so exciting, and because you were so dedicated, I wondered if maybe I would like it as much as you. But it's your dream, and I don't think you should give it up." Melissa gave me an exasperated look. "That's why," she said emphatically.

"Oh." I felt stunned. Melissa admired me? Since when? "Why didn't you tell me all this when you wanted to join? I wouldn't have gotten so mad."

"Because," Melissa said, "I thought you were being a spoiled brat, and I didn't feel like telling you what a great swimmer I thought you were."

I felt suddenly ashamed. "Mel, I'm really sorry. I thought you were trying to grab all the attention, just like always … I mean, how I felt you always did. I thought you wanted to take the one thing I was good at and prove you were better at that, too."

Melissa shook her head. "No. I just wanted to be part of it, too. Mom and Dad are always so impressed with you and the team. You just never seem to notice."

"They are?"

"Yeah." Melissa was silent for a moment. "So, what about the swim team?" she asked. "Can I help you pay the fees?"

I sighed. "Mel, I appreciate the offer, but you don't have enough money. For the amount of money I'd need, you and I would have to deliver about forty million flyers every day."

"Is it that expensive? My fees weren't."

"That's because you weren't in the competitive program. Believe me, with paying for pool time, plus competition registrations and suits and equipment — it's a lot more money than we have."

"Oh." Disappointment showed on Melissa's face. "That's lousy. I thought I'd solved the problem for you."

I stood up, and did something I hadn't done in years. I gave Melissa a hug. "That's the nicest thing you've ever done for me."

Melissa looked startled, but she hugged me back. We both felt awkward for a minute, then Melissa cleared her throat. "So what are we going to do about the swim team?"

I shrugged helplessly. "I guess I'll have to talk to Mom and Dad."

12

Something to Talk About

Hey, Jo-Jo," Mom said cheerfully. She poured batter into the waffle iron. "We're having waffles with some fresh fruit for dinner, as a special treat."

I glanced at the ripe strawberries, fresh pineapple, and buttery slices of papaya resting on the counter. Dad, who was washing the strawberries, looked relaxed and happy for the first time in weeks.

"What are we celebrating?" I asked. I dipped a fingertip into the batter and tasted it. Breakfast food for dinner was Melissa's favourite — she loved bacon and eggs, or pancakes with hash browns, or waffles instead of the beef stews and pastas that I loved. I felt a twinge of annoyance, but I pushed it aside. There were more important things I wanted to talk about.

"We are celebrating ..." Dad paused dramatically, holding a pitcher of juice aloft. "Me! Your old Dad solved the unemployment problem today. At least, I think so."

"Really?" I asked eagerly. "What happened?"

"Well, I've decided to go into business for myself," Dad said. He began pouring the juice. "I found another client today, and between that and my contract work with the old company, some money will be trickling in. And I figure that if I work at it, well, there's lots of people who need advertising work done. I think I can build up a pretty decent income."

"That's great, Dad." I tried to sound enthusiastic, but Dad's news didn't change anything for me. I was glad, of course, that he was happy, but we still didn't have much money, and that meant I would still have to quit the swim team.

Mom opened the waffle iron, and a sweet, steamy vanilla smell rose into the air.

"Mmmm," Melissa poked her head around the kitchen door. "What's for dinner?"

"Your favourite," I said. "Waffles."

"Yum!" said Melissa. She gave me an inquiring look. I shook my head slightly, to tell her that I hadn't said anything to Mom and Dad yet. Melissa frowned and made a nudging gesture with her chin, as if to say, "Well, hurry up."

I was about to make a face at her, but Mom interrupted.

"What's all the nodding and twitching about?" She'd been watching us.

"Oh, nothing," I said.

Melissa frowned again. "Josie ..." she said.

"Josie, what?" Mom asked. She looked much too interested to be distracted easily.

"I ... um ... have something I need to talk to you and Dad about," I said.

Melissa gave me a thumbs-up sign and backed out of the kitchen. I took a fresh grip on my courage.

"What's up, honey?" Mom turned the heat on the waffle iron down low and sat down at the table. Dad returned the juice to the fridge and pulled up his chair. They both looked at me and waited.

This concern was overwhelming. I usually felt like I had to drop an anvil on someone's foot to get any attention.

"Um ..." I thought about telling them how I'd single-handedly made history with the Great Science Fair Disaster but decided to break that news later. As hard as it was, I needed to talk about how I felt. "Well … the thing is …" I stopped. I didn't have a clue how to begin.

"Go on, honey," Mom encouraged.

"Well, how come you love Melissa more than me?" I blurted. I didn't even think about the words, they just flew out of my mouth.

Mom and Dad looked thunderstruck. "What?" they said.

"How come you love Melissa more? She's the one who always gets all your attention. She gets better grades than me, she's prettier than me, she's friendlier and more popular than me — it's bad enough that everyone at school always notices Melissa, and I'm just known as her twerpy little sister, but when my own parents never even seem to think I exist …" My voice squeaked, and I stopped, embarrassed.

"Josie," Mom's voice was soft, and she put an arm around my shoulder, "we love you very much, just as much as we love Melissa. Why would you think that we don't?"

"Well," I tried to steady my voice, "you always make a big deal when Melissa gets a good report card or has some dance recital or band show or something. Nobody seems to get excited about anything I do. I'm just not good at stuff like Melissa is."

Mom and Dad exchanged glances.

"But Josie," Dad tried to interrupt.

I shook my head and kept going. I had a list of grievances that had been bottled up for a long time, and I wasn't going to stop now.

"And you make her favourite foods to celebrate things, she never gets yelled at, and she always gets new clothes. I just have to wear her old things half the time."

"Okay, hold on," Mom stopped me firmly. "Let's backtrack a bit. Tonight we made waffles to celebrate Dad's new idea. True, Melissa loves waffles, but who else in this family can eat them by the pile?"

I thought for a minute. Dad loved waffles with brown-sugar syrup and pecans. One Sunday morning I thought he was going to explode, he consumed so many.

"Dad, I guess," I said.

Dad looked sheepish. "I don't really eat them by the pile, you know."

Mom gestured for him to keep quiet. "Right. Dad does. So I made them for him and Melissa. But I've never known you to complain about them, either."

I shrugged. "I guess."

"Now about clothes, it saves money for us to pass Melissa's clothes on to you. It has nothing to do with us loving Melissa more. Besides, I seem to remember going shopping with you last summer and buying a whole stack of brand-new stuff just for you."

I stared at my fingernails. "Yeah," I said.

"And Josie, how often do Dad and I get up in the morning to take you to swim practice?"

"Four times a week," I said.

"And how many competitions do we go to, to see you swim?"

I thought about it. "Almost all, I guess. Except the out-of-town ones."

"Right," Mom said. "And even for those, Dad or I have volunteered to drive many times, just so we could be there with you. Josie, you're so busy concentrating on what attention Melissa gets, and what she's good at, that you forget what's special about you."

"Maybe." I felt like crying. Everything Mom said was true, but so far it didn't make me feel any better. Then she reached over and stroked my hair.

"Josie," she said. "You are very, very important to us. We love you very much. And you have talents of your own. I don't know another person who has the dedication to practise swimming the way you do."

"Yeah, Jo. That kind of training would put me in traction," Dad said.

I managed a watery smile.

"We are very proud of you, Josie," Dad said seriously. "You're a great swimmer. We know we'll see you standing up on those podiums some day."

"Not any more," I whispered.

"What are you talking about?" Mom said.

"Well, we don't have much money with Dad not working at the agency. And my swimming fees went way up this year. So we can't afford it. I can't swim any more. I won't even be able to go to the competition next week."

"Whoa. Hold everything," Dad exclaimed. "Jo, we never said you'd have to quit."

"I figured it out for myself."

"Well, you figured wrong. We never intended to stop paying for you to swim."

"I thought it was an unnecessary expenditure," I said.

"It's not. It's a very necessary expenditure," Mom said. "Because it's important to you. We told Melissa she'd have to use her flyer-route money to pay if she wanted to join the non-competitive club because it's just a fun hobby for her, and that's the kind of thing we have to cut down on."

"Besides, Josie, there's all the fund-raising projects this year. You and Mom and I — maybe even Melissa, too — can cut your fees in half by making use of them. I already talked to Dale about it," said Dad.

"You did?"

"Sure." Dad squeezed my shoulder. "Why didn't you just ask us about it? We would have told you."

"I was scared," I confessed. "I didn't want to hear you tell me I couldn't swim."

Mom shook her head. "Josie, you keep too much inside. If you'd just open up a little, you might find that the things that are bothering you aren't so bad after all."

"Yeah," I said.

Dad hugged me. "We would have told you how much we loved you, if we'd known how you were feeling. But I guess we just assumed everything was okay because you never said anything. I'm sorry for that, Jo."

"Me, too," Mom said. She reached out to pat my hand.

"Okay, let's not get too mushy about this." Melissa popped into the kitchen. "And I'm starved. Are those waffles ready yet?"

I wiped my nose with the back of my sleeve and grinned at her. "Now you're talking!" I said.

13

Winner Takes All

Loosen up!" I whispered. I shrugged my shoulders vigorously and began some slow windmill circles with my arms to ease the tension.

The day of the Calgary invitational swim meet had finally arrived. It was always nice to have a swim meet in our home pool, but today it was so crowded with kids, coaches, parents, team warm-up suits, and swim bags that it looked like a different place.

Melissa, Mom, Dad, and Delaney were somewhere up in the bleachers. Melissa, of course, wasn't swimming. This meet was for the competitive swimmers, and besides, she needed a lot more training before she would be ready to compete.

"Hey, Josie," Dale hurried over. "How are you feeling?"

"Great!" I forced a bright smile from my nervous lips.

Dale saw right through me. "Don't be scared. It's just another meet, like all the others. You've swum these races hundreds of times."

"I know, but this time I actually have a chance to win."

"Josie, you can do it. You've trained hard. You've cut your time down in practice and you can do it here. Just concentrate. Don't think about the other swimmers. Okay?"

I nodded, but I couldn't help thinking about the swimmers from the other clubs. There were so many who were fast. How could I hope to beat them? I was just a good, solid swimmer who worked really, really hard. I wasn't naturally talented like Melissa.

Dale was still looking at me and seemed to read my mind, because he said, "It's up here, Josie." He tapped his temple with a forefinger. "Talent can only take you so far. The rest is up here. Winning is up here. Some swimmers who are incredibly talented crumble under pressure, or can't take the demands of training, or fail to concentrate when it counts." Dale grasped both my shoulders and swivelled me so he could look right into my eyes.

"You've got what it takes, Josie. I've seen that winning edge before, and you have it. Believe me, I know."

The intensity of his words left me spellbound. I stared at Dale, dazed.

Dale grinned. "So go warm up. It's almost time to race."

I took a deep breath and walked to the pool edge. The water felt warm against my toes, and my whole body tingled with anticipation. Other swimmers were already in the lanes, and I found one that wasn't too crowded, pulled on my swim cap and goggles, and plunged in.

The water's coolness flowed in sleek ripples over my skin, and my strokes felt long and smooth and strong. Butterfly suddenly seemed easy, almost effortless. I swam 200 metres, then switched to freestyle until my muscles felt warm and loose, and all the tension was gone.

The pool was emptying. I pulled myself out of the water, wrapped a towel and my club jacket around me to keep my muscles warm, and sat down to wait. I was swimming several different races, but the 200 butterfly was my first one, and it wasn't scheduled for a while.

I blotted the back of my neck with the towel and briskly massaged my shoulder muscles with my fingertips. I felt the muscles relax, looked up, and felt them tense all over again.

Melissa was leaning over the bleacher railing, talking intently to Dale. Her blond wavy hair fell in a cascade over her shoulder, and she looked confident, gesturing as she talked.

A pang of jealousy swept through me. Melissa still managed to attract attention, even when she wasn't participating on a day as important as this.

I sighed. It was so hard to stop feeling envious. Even though I told myself that there was no reason to feel upset, I still did. I tried to remind myself that Melissa was no different than Ross or Joanne or Beth from the team — and Dale paid attention to all of them. I never felt jealous of any of the other swimmers. Just Melissa.

But then I stopped myself. This was my day. I was here to compete, and I needed to concentrate. If Melissa wanted to swim on the team or won praise from Dale, it didn't make me any better or worse as a swimmer. Only I could do that. With that thought came a feeling of relief. I was back in control.

Dale laughed at something Melissa said, then moved on to give some last minute instructions to Ross. I did a few stretches and began to mentally rehearse each part of my butterfly stroke.

"Psst! Josie!" The voice came from the bleachers, and when I looked up, Melissa was motioning for me to come over. I took a deep breath.

"I wanted to wish you luck," she said.

"Thanks." I smiled at her. "I'm really glad you came." And I meant it.

"I couldn't miss watching my little sister kick some serious butt," Melissa said. "Oh, and Mom and Dad thought your adventure at the science fair was really funny."

"You told them?" I squeaked. "How could you?"

She reached over the railing and noogied the top of my swim cap. "I'm kidding, bozo. You can tell them, if you want to some time."

"Maybe when I'm thirty," I said.

"Swim hard." Melissa retreated back into the bleachers to sit with Mom and Dad.

"I will," I whispered. Mom and Dad flashed me encouraging smiles and Delaney gave me a thumbs-up sign. I walked slowly back to the team, where Dale was helping the younger swimmers work on stretches before their heats.

The next race was 200-metre butterfly. The swimmers in the water for 100-metre breast stroke strained for the edge, and I watched them as I shook my shoulders loose and tightened my goggle strap. I wasn't taking any chances that my goggles might fall off on the dive.

Because this was a small meet, the officials were only running one heat of each race. Usually in a big meet there are preliminary heats, and then the swimmers with the top eight times go on to qualify for the final heat. Then they swim the race a second time, and the swimmer with the top time in that race is the winner. But in this competition, we only had one heat for each race. That meant there were no second chances.

I found out which lane I was supposed to be in, while an official announced the race. I went to the starting block in lane five, tugged my swim cap down more securely, and swung my arms in a few wide circles.

Then I stepped up to the block. The swimmers in the other seven lanes wore tense expressions, but I felt strangely relaxed. I fastened my goggles on securely and planted my feet in a good, strong stance for my dive.

The pool and bleachers fell silent. I looked out across the water. It gleamed like smooth glass. I exhaled slowly.

"Take your marks!" The announcer's voice sounded loud and metallic through the microphone.

I bent forward and gripped the edge of the starting block. My thighs tensed, waiting for the signal.

BEEP!

I exploded from the starting block. My dive was shallow and long, which helped me gain some speed. I concentrated on strong, powerful strokes and I hit the pool edge after the first lap so quickly it surprised me. I made a knife-sharp turn and plowed on.

By the fourth lap my arms began to feel tired, and I had to concentrate hard on my breathing. I felt like I was gulping air every time I came up for a breath, instead of breathing easily. I struggled to breathe smoothly, and I remembered what Dale had told me about my kick. I pushed my legs harder, flicking my feet downward, and that extra speed gave my arms a bit of a rest.

The last lap. Blood rushed in my ears. Dimly I could hear a lot of screaming whenever my head came out of the water. I wondered what was going on. I couldn't see any one ahead of me, but it was hard to tell through the churning water and my now-foggy goggles.

I slashed my arms through the water with as much speed as I could muster. My legs whipped through each kick with all my strength.

I stretched for the edge. My fingers touched the tiles and I came up, gasping. I ripped off my goggles and searched the scoreboard for my time. I was first! I'd won!

But what was all the yelling about? I looked around in bewilderment as the other swimmers kicked in to the finish. Parents in the bleachers were applauding, and my own mother and father were whooping and hollering like lunatics. Delaney was standing on the bench, waving both fists in the air, and Melissa was leaning on the bleacher railing, jumping up and down.

Then Dale reached over the starting block and hauled me out of the pool.

"Josie, you did it!" He swung me off my feet. "I can't believe it! I've never seen you swim like that before."

"It felt like a terrific swim," I said.

"It should!" Dale answered. "You broke the provincial record for your age category! You cut two-tenths of a second off the time for 200-metre butterfly. I've never seen such a beautiful race in my whole life."

"Really?" A bright, tingly feeling gradually spread through my whole body, and a wide smile glued itself to my face. "Wow! I really broke the record?"

"You better believe it. Congratulations, kiddo." Dale squeezed my shoulder, and then a flood of kids from the team surrounded me. Ross thumped me on the back, and I was hugged and congratulated by almost everyone.

I couldn't believe it. Me, Josie Waterson — I broke the provincial record. That meant my name would be written up as the new record holder, and I would probably get to go to Nationals, if I could swim that fast again at Provincials. I couldn't wait!

The race officials were having a hard time getting the swim meet back on schedule. Gradually the crowd around me thinned. I looked up to the bleachers, into the beaming eyes of my mom and dad. Then I looked at Melissa. Her face lit up and she cupped her hands around her mouth.

"Way to go, sis!" she yelled, ignoring the disapproving stares from the race officials.

I grinned. I had just achieved the biggest accomplishment of my whole life. And I was glad that Melissa was there to share it with me.